This is a delightful story that is for the entire family to enjoy.

Monster Family's Little Troubles is a fictional story. This book can be used to bring joy and for you to bond with your little ones.

This book has fun and colorful illustrations by Leroy Grayson that will make this book come to life and it's guaranteed to bring a smile to your child's face.

This book is dedicated to my two beautiful kids

John and Faith Otah

I want to say thank you, Leroy Grayson, for his ability to illustrate my vision.

Also, my publisher Anelda Attaway aka Jazzy Kitty, the CEO of Jazzy Kitty Publications.

Monster Family's Little Troubles

By Stanley Otah

Illustrations by Leroy Grayson

Published by Jazzy Kitty Publications

New Castle, DE 19720

877.782.5550 - http://www.jazzykittypublications.com

anelda@jazzykittypublications.com

Copyright © 2020 Stanley Otah

ISBN 978-1-954425-02-6

Library of Congress Control Number: 2020925305

Credits: Cover image and illustrations by Leroy Grayson of Quality Pictures qualitypictures2@aol.com; Book Cover created and Editing by Anelda Attaway Co-editor Leroy Grayson; Logo Designs by Andre M. Saunders and Jess Zimmerman.

All rights explicitly reserved worldwide. This book is protected under the copyright laws of the United States of America. This book may not be copied or reprinted for commercial profit or net income. The purpose of short quotations or occasional page copying for personal or group study is permitted and promoted. Permission to copy will be freely granted upon request for Worldwide Distribution, printed, and published in the United States of America. Created Jazzy Kitty Greetings Marketing & Publishing, LLC dba Jazzy Kitty Publications are utilizing Microsoft Publishing and BookCoverly Software.

A Fictional Story

MONSTER FAMILY'S LITTLE TROUBLES

BY STANLY OTAH

Illustrations by Leroy Grayson

This is a story that begins as the Monster Family "Daddy Monster, Mommy Monster, Girl Monster, and Boy Monster" sits down to eat dinner; they had ice cream, cake, donuts, and milk.

Big Daddy Monster was upset that Girl Monster was being bad at school. They made fun of her and made her feel sad. They called her STINKY.

"Don't worry about them," said Mommy Monster, "you don't smell." Then Mommy Monster asked Girl Monster, "Why were you bad in school?"

She quickly answered, "They made fun of me and called me stinky and ugly."

"Don't listen to them; you're beautiful to me," said Mommy Monster.

The next day after school, Girl Monster asked, "May I go out to play?"

Daddy monster said, "Yes."

And as soon as she started to play, her friends started making fun of her again.

She yelled and told them, "My Mom said if you don't leave me alone, she is going to come out here and eat you!"

Her three friends ran home, crying, "They going to eat us!"

Mom Monster called Girl Monster and asked her, "Why did your friends run away?"

"I told them if they didn't leave me alone, you were going to eat them."

"I'm not going to eat them; don't you go around telling story's."

The next day, Girl Monster and Boy Monster went to school.

Her friends made fun of her again and pulled her hair.

"My Daddy said leave me alone, or he will come down here and eat you."

The teacher put her in time out and made her write, *"I will not tell story's 100 times."*

"I'm going to tell my Daddy you hit me."

"I will tell your Mother how you are behaving."

When Girl Monster got home, her mother was very upset with her.

"You have been bad again. I want you to stop telling story's or I won't let you go out to play."

Girl Monster then said, "I won't be bad anymore."

"Ok, we'll see."

Boy Monster is playing ball with his friend, and the friend takes his ball and runs away.

He yelled, "Bring my ball back, or I will tell my Daddy to eat you!"

His friend quickly gave him his ball back because he did not want to be eaten.

The next day, they wanted to go out and play, but it was raining. Their friends were outside playing, and they wanted to play too.

They were allowed to go out, so they put on their hats, coats, and boots. The kids were having such a good time, so they took off their hats, coats, and boots to splash and jump in the rain. They had a great time until their mother called them inside.

The next day, they could not go to school because they were sick from playing in the rain.

Mom Monster took their temperature, gave them cold medicine and Chicken Noodle Soup; they slept all day.

When they woke up, they felt much better.

The next day, Mom Monster got them up for school, and since they felt better, they wanted to go.

After school, their friends came over because they missed making fun of them and wanted them to come out and play.

Daddy Monster came home and their friends saw him and were afraid he would eat them.

So they ran from the house crying because he was big, hairy, and scary.

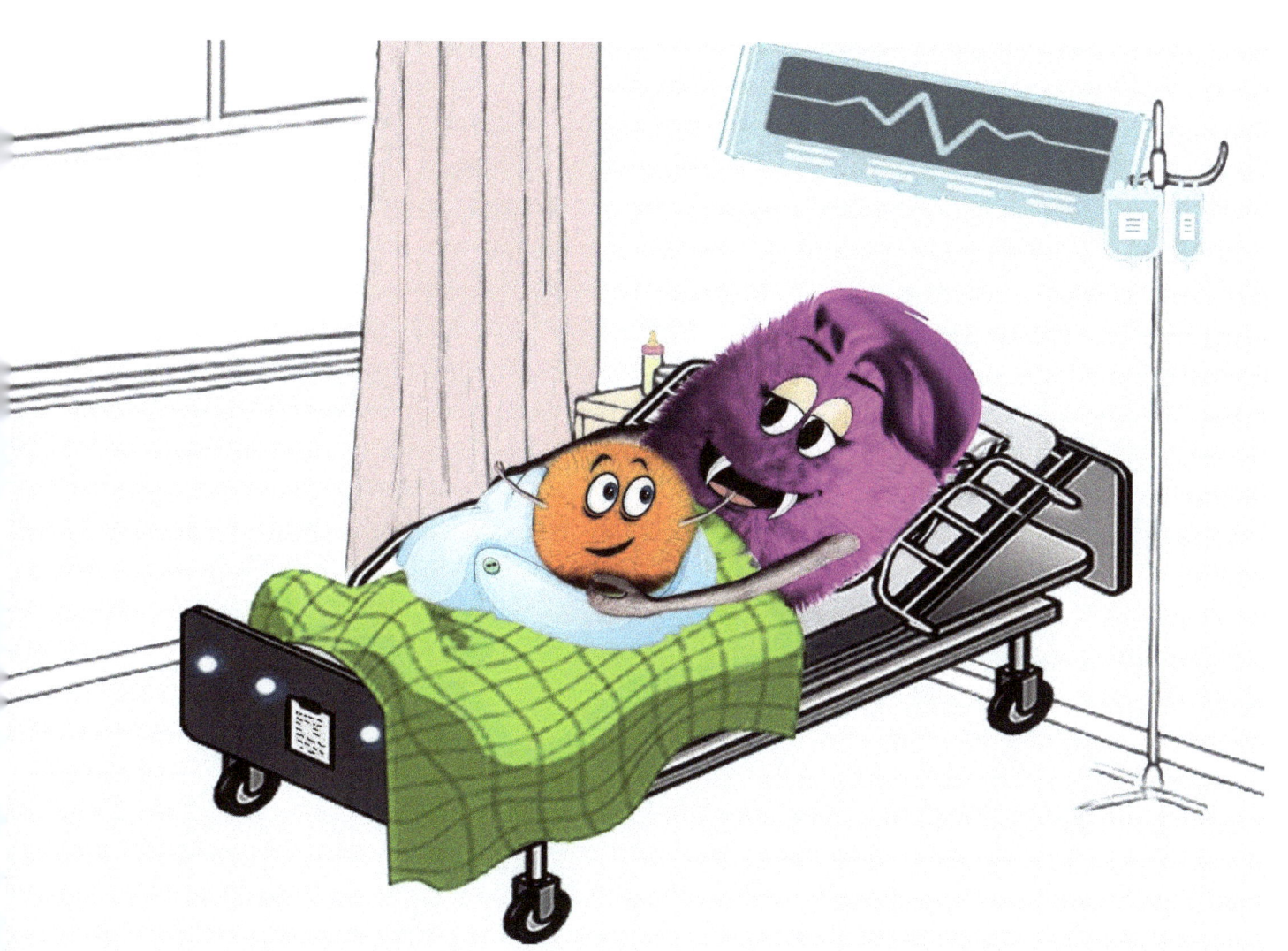

Mommy Monster had a little Baby Monster and he was orange.

The Baby Monster was furry and looked exactly like them.

The next day, Daddy Monster wanted to make up for scaring their friends. So he had a big party and invited them all. They had Ice cream, cookies, cake, potato chips, and all kinds of goodies and they were yummy. They also played games, put on birthday hats, and had a good time getting their bellies full.

Everybody thanked Daddy Monster for all the snacks that he gave them. Daddy Monster might look scary, but he's just a big, cuddly, furry Daddy Monster with a big heart.

Daddy Monster likes little kids and would never do anything to harm or hurt them.

The End

www.ingramcontent.com/pod-product-compliance
Lightning Source LLC
Chambersburg PA
CBHW041232240426
43673CB00010B/313